For my Mom

Whose creativity continues
to be my inspiration.

The Magic Sceptre ™
Reginald the Rabbit
Text and Illustrations
Copyright © 2007 Joan K. Creamer
Printed in China
For information address
Silver Snowflake Publishing.
P.O. Box 1256, East Greenwich, RI 02818
www.TheMagicSceptre.com
Second Edition
3 5 7 9 10 8 6 4 2
SAN: 8 5 0 - 3 9 4 X

Publisher's Cataloging-in-Publication
(Provided by Quality Books, Inc.)

Creamer, Joan Klatil.
   The magic sceptre. Reginald the Rabbit / written and
illustrated by Joan Klatil Creamer.
      p. cm.
   SUMMARY: Explains the special magic that allows a
family of rabbits to make holiday treats during the
Easter season and how the Easter egg hunt began with the
help of The Magic Sceptre and Reginald the Rabbit.
   Audience: Ages 3-9.
   ISBN-13: 978-0-9778476-5-5
   ISBN-10: 0-9778476-5-9

   1. Easter--Juvenile fiction. 2. Easter Bunny--
Juvenile fiction. 3. Magic--Juvenile fiction.
[1. Easter--Fiction. 2. Easter Bunny--Fiction.
3. Magic--Fiction. 7. Rabbits--Fiction.   I. Title.
II. Title: Reginald the Rabbit.

PZ7.C85985Magr 2007   [E]
                      QBI07-600217

The Magic Sceptre

Reginald the Rabbit

For Eva
Enjoy the Magic!
Joan Klatil Creamer

Written and Illustrated by
Joan Klatil Creamer

After a long, cold winter boys and girls look forward to the arrival of spring. This season brings Easter, egg hunts and baskets full of treats.

What most people don't know is that the rabbits of
Carrotville look forward to Easter as well. You see, the job
of preparing for Easter is passed down from one honored
rabbit family to another. This particular year Mr. and Mrs.
Harvey Hare and their children, Rudy, Randall, Radcliff,
Hailey, Hannah and Harriet were the chosen family.

The Hare family was excited,
but there was so much
to do! They had eggs to decorate,
chocolate bunnies to mold and
jellybeans to make. But the best
part of Easter was seeing the
children's happy faces when they saw
their colorful baskets. The Hare family
went right to work.

Hannah collected eggs to decorate. Soon she learned that chickens lay only one egg each day. "That means we won't have enough eggs by Easter," she sighed.

Randall put a large pot of chocolate on the stove to make the chocolate bunnies. When he tried to form a bunny, the gooey chocolate ran all over the kitchen floor. "What a mess!" he said.

Hailey, the fashion expert, was going to pick the colors for the jellybeans. Soon she was distracted. "This fashion magazine dress matches my eyes," she remarked.

When Radcliff and Harriet practiced hopping with springs on their feet they couldn't control their bouncing. "We'll never deliver the baskets of treats on time!" they sobbed.

"What should we do?"
cried Mr. and Mrs. Hare.
"We'll never be ready for Easter!"
Everyone was worried.

"Reginald the Rabbit can help us.
He can use the powers of the Magic Sceptre."
said Rudy, the youngest of the Hare family.

"Really, Rudy?" cried Hailey and Hannah together.
"Wow! You could save Easter this year." So off they
hopped with Rudy leading the way to Reginald's carrot house.

Being the oldest and wisest rabbit in all of Carrotville, Reginald was the only one able to borrow The Magic Sceptre from...

Santa Claus at the North Pole. As he gave them the Magic Sceptre,
Santa Claus shared the secret words that make the Magic Sceptre work.

Since this is the holiday of eggs, the snowflake on top of The Magic Sceptre turned into a beautiful glowing crystal egg as Reginald and Rudy carried The Magic Sceptre to Carrotville.

"Hmmmmm, now what were those magic words again?"
mumbled Reginald.

Rudy rushed up to Reginald and whispered in his ear. Smiling, Reginald tapped the Magic Sceptre three times and said, "Let every child believe in the Easter Bunny and the magic that happens at Easter."... POOF!!!

A Magic rainbow with colored chicken feed, candy molds, pogo sticks and jars of jelly appeared!

Hannah fed the magic, colored chicken feed to
the chickens. Not only did they lay MORE eggs but
they were DECORATED eggs. "Yippee!" shouted Hannah.

Randall discovered making chocolate bunnies
was a lot easier when you had candy forms to shape the chocolate.
"Mmmmmmmmm!" said Rudy sampling a chocolate bunny.

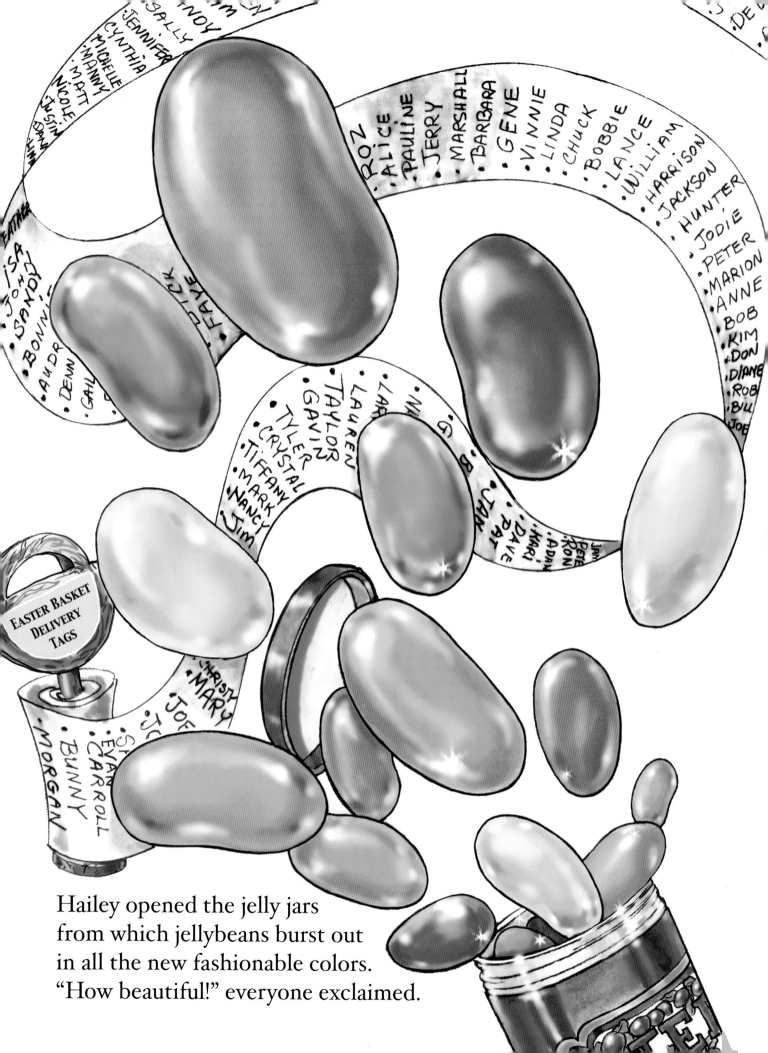

Hailey opened the jelly jars
from which jellybeans burst out
in all the new fashionable colors.
"How beautiful!" everyone exclaimed.

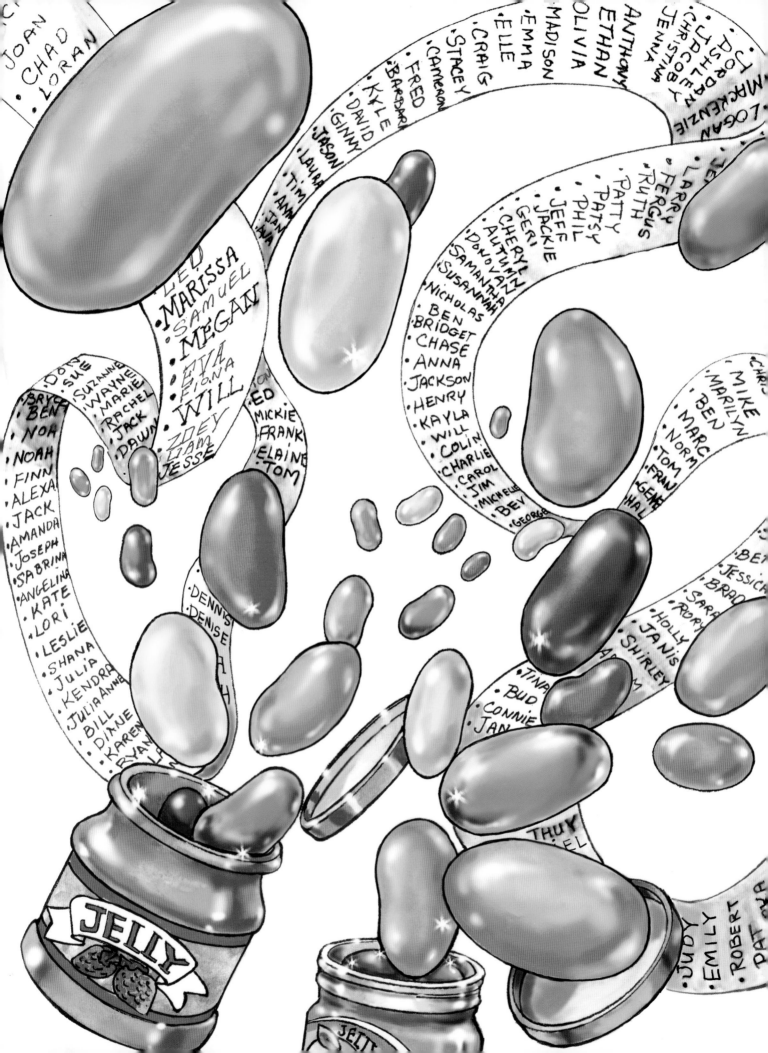

With the help of The Magic Sceptre, Radcliff and Harriet used their new pogo sticks to deliver the Easter baskets faster than anyone ever had ever done before.

Reginald and Rudy noticed a few eggs had fallen out of the baskets that were being delivered. They had an idea, but would need a sign to hang in the tree.

The Hare family was very happy. Thanks to Rudy, Reginald and The Magic Sceptre, it had been the best Easter ever.

When the celebration came to an end, Reginald returned
The Magic Sceptre to the North Pole. Its magic powers might
be needed for another holiday.

Now you know The Legend of
the Easter Bunny and
the Magic Sceptre.

Happy Easter